This book belongs to

_____

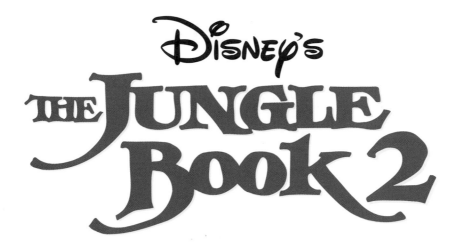

A READ-ALOUD STORYBOOK

Adapted by Catherine Hapka
Illustrated by Judith Clarke, Lori Tyminski
and the Disney Storybook Artists
Designed by Disney's Global Design Group

Random House 🏠 New York

Copyright © 2003 Disney Enterprises, Inc. Based on the Mowgli Stories in *The Jungle Book* and *The Second Jungle Book* by Rudyard Kipling. All rights reserved under International and Pan-American Copyright Conventions. Published in the United States by Random House Children's Books, a division of Random House, Inc., New York, and simultaneously in Canada by Random House of Canada Limited, Toronto, in conjunction with Disney Enterprises, Inc. RANDOM HOUSE and colophon are registered trademarks of Random House, Inc.
Library of Congress Catalog Number: 2002107817 ISBN: 0-7364-2084-3
www.randomhouse.com/kids/disney
Printed in the United States of America
10 9 8 7 6 5 4 3 2 1

The Man-Village

Mowgli wasn't sure about life in the Man-village. Sure, the village leader and his wife treated Mowgli like a son. And he even had a new four-year-old brother, Ranjan. But he had to do so many chores and obey so many rules!

Mowgli often missed his carefree days in the jungle. He liked telling stories about his adventures and performing puppet shows for his new friends and family—although sometimes Ranjan got in the way.

Mowgli's new friend Shanti liked hearing his stories. But sometimes he and Ranjan would try to scare her with tales of the wild jungle.

One morning, Mowgli and Ranjan raced down to the river. They arrived seconds before Shanti did.

"What are *you* doing here?" she asked Mowgli.

"I'm on the lookout," Mowgli told her. "Yesterday I saw tiger tracks *right here*! So watch your back, or the last thing you'll ever hear is—"

"*ROAAARRR!*" Ranjan yelled, leaping out of the bushes.

Shanti screamed and dropped her water jug. "You're horrible, horrible stinky boys!" she cried. "C'mon, Ranjan. He's a bad influence," she said, dragging the young boy away.

Mowgli felt bad about scaring Shanti, so he brought the water jug back to her. Then he decided to show her and Ranjan a clever trick he had learned in the jungle. He shot a banana out of its peel and right into Ranjan's mouth.

"Well, here's a little trick I learned right here at home," Shanti said. She tossed a mango into the air. It caught on a branch and peeled itself on the way down.

"Wow, that's a neater trick!" Ranjan cried.

Moments later, Mowgli started dancing to the jungle rhythms from across the river. Ranjan and the other village children joined in. Even Shanti couldn't help dancing along.

Suddenly, she realized where Mowgli was leading them. "Wait!" she cried. "Stop! You're crossing the river! You can't go into the jungle!"

Ranjan's father heard Shanti's cries. He called the children back, then scolded Mowgli. "The jungle is a dangerous place," he said. He rolled up his sleeve to show Mowgli the scars on his arm— scars from a tiger's claws. "I should know."

Later, Mowgli stared out his window at the jungle in the distance. "Oh, Baloo," he whispered. How he missed his best friend!

At that same moment, out in the jungle, Baloo the bear was missing Mowgli. He tried to build a Man-cub out of plants and a coconut, but it just wasn't the same.

Bagheera the panther watched Baloo. "Poor fellow," he murmured.

As Baloo and Bagheera wandered off, a shadow fell across the clearing. It was Shere Khan, the tiger! His huge paw came down hard, crushing the fake Mowgli head.

Shere Khan was still angry at Mowgli for burning his tail with a fiery branch. He wanted revenge! All he had to do was find the Man-cub.

Meanwhile, Baloo decided it was time to find his little buddy. He set off for the Man-village.

Bagheera stepped in front of him. "It's not safe for Mowgli in the jungle," he said. "You know Shere Khan is looking for him."

But Baloo wouldn't listen—not even Colonel Hathi and his elephant troops could stop him from going to the Man-village.

As Baloo entered the Man-village, he had no idea that Shere Khan was close behind him.

"Papa Bear! Boy, am I glad to see you!" Mowgli cried when he saw his friend. He and Baloo gave each other a big hug. Then the happy pair began playing the way they used to in the jungle.

Shanti arrived just in time to see the reunion. She thought Baloo was a wild bear—and that he was attacking Mowgli!

"Help!" she screamed. "There's a wild animal in the village!" Startled, Baloo grabbed Mowgli and ran away.

The villagers rushed out and spotted . . . Shere Khan! They quickly chased the tiger out of the village.

Shanti was confused. Why wasn't anyone helping her save Mowgli from that vicious bear? She chased Baloo and Mowgli herself—all the way across the river and into the jungle! Ranjan was the only one who saw her go.

Back in the Jungle

Kaa spotted Baloo and Mowgli as they wandered into the jungle.

"Do my *sssnake eyesss* deceive me?" he said. "It's the *sssucculent Man-cub!*"

Unaware of the snake, Baloo licked some tasty ants from the bottom of a rock. Then he tossed the rock to Mowgli.

"Thanks, Baloo." Mowgli licked off a few ants, then threw the rock over his shoulder. It hit Kaa right in the head!

As Shanti searched for Mowgli, Kaa spotted her, too. But Ranjan appeared just in time to save Shanti from the hungry snake. "Bad snake!" Ranjan shouted, beating Kaa with a stick.

Moments later, Shere Khan found Kaa lying dazed on the ground. "Where is the Man-cub?" the tiger demanded.

Kaa didn't know where Mowgli had gone, but he didn't want to make Shere Khan angry. "He'sss at the ssswamp!" he fibbed.

So Shere Khan set off for the swamp just as the villagers reached the jungle in search of the three missing children.

Colonel Hathi and his elephant troops panicked when they heard the humans. They were afraid the humans were there to go hunting.

"Man is in the jungle!" Colonel Hathi cried.

As a group of villagers passed nearby, Bagheera saw that the elephant was right.

"Shanti! Ranjan!" a woman called.

"Mowgli!" Ranjan's father cried.

Suddenly, Bagheera realized why the villagers were there. "Baloo . . . ," he muttered.

Mowgli had no idea he was causing such trouble. He tossed a mango into the air, just as Shanti had done back at the village. It peeled itself on a tree branch on the way down.

"Not bad!" Baloo said. "Where'd you learn to do that?"

"Shanti showed me," Mowgli replied.

"Shanti?" Baloo repeated suspiciously. He was a little jealous that Mowgli had a new friend.

Just then Bagheera arrived. "What are you doing out here, Baggy?" Baloo asked, hiding Mowgli behind him.

"Man is in the jungle," Bagheera replied grimly. "They're searching for Mowgli."

"Wow," Mowgli said after Bagheera left. "The whole village—looking for me? I wonder if Shanti's with them."

"Shanti?" Baloo exclaimed. "You definitely don't want her to find you, do ya?"

Mowgli realized his old friend was right—he didn't need his human friends anymore. He made Baloo promise to scare Shanti away if she ever caught up with them. Baloo agreed, and the pair practiced their scaring.

Shanti was worried. She and Ranjan were lost. She made a map of sticks and stones to help them figure out where they were.

"Okay, here's the village," she muttered. "We crossed the river and . . . um . . ."

As Shanti rearranged some of the stones, Ranjan spotted a coil of mango peel nearby.

Shanti gasped when she saw the peel. "It's Mowgli! He must have been here!" she shouted.

On his search for Mowgli, Shere Khan had just reached the swamp. But there was no sign of the Man-cub.

"That snake lied to me!" Shere Khan growled.

Some vultures were watching him. "We heard that kid is right here in the jungle, right under your whiskers," one of them told Shere Khan. "They say he's headed downriver with a bear."

"Downriver, you say?" The tiger smiled wickedly and dashed off.

Meanwhile, Baloo took Mowgli to an old temple. As a baboon band started to play, Baloo and Mowgli danced off into the crowd.

After the dance was over, a monkey asked Mowgli, "They don't swing out like that in your Man-village, now, do they, kid?"

"He told me all about that scene," Baloo interrupted. "They've got rules, rules, rules!"

Mowgli started to feel bad. They made it sound as if the Man-village were a terrible place to live!

Mowgli slipped away from Baloo and the others. He found a tree branch with a view of the Man-village and climbed onto it to think.

Staring at the village, he wondered where he really belonged. He missed Shanti and Ranjan and his other friends in the village. But he didn't want to leave Baloo and his friends in the jungle. What was he supposed to do?

Finding Mowgli

As Shanti and Ranjan continued searching for Mowgli, they heard sad humming up ahead.

"Mowgli!" Ranjan cried happily.

He and Shanti found their friend sitting in a tree. Mowgli was so surprised and excited to see them that he slipped and got tangled in some vines.

"What are you doing out here?" he asked Shanti.

"We came to save you," Shanti explained.

Seconds later, Baloo appeared. The bear gasped. "It's her!" He remembered that Mowgli wanted him to scare Shanti away.

"ROOOOOOAAAAAAARRRR!" Baloo charged toward them.

"Baloo, don't!" Mowgli cried.

But it was too late. Ranjan screamed in terror.

Suddenly, the bear tripped on a vine. It wrapped around his leg, tangling *him* just like Mowgli.

Shanti was scared. But she was angry, too. She stepped up and punched Baloo right in the nose.

Mowgli felt terrible. This was all his fault!

All of a sudden, Shanti realized what was going on. "You planned this?" she demanded, glaring at Mowgli.

"No!" Mowgli cried. "Shanti, I can explain!"

Shanti grabbed Ranjan and stormed off. Mowgli chased after them, leaving Baloo behind.

Mowgli caught up with Shanti a moment later. Her eyes were wide and frightened. Mowgli turned—and saw Shere Khan slinking toward them!

The tiger chuckled. "You seem surprised to see me, Man-cub."

Mowgli jumped in front of Shanti and Ranjan, trying to protect them.

"*Run!*" Mowgli whispered to his friends.

Mowgli, Shanti, and Ranjan ran through the jungle until they found a hiding place in some overgrown bushes. "Stay here!" Mowgli told them.

"Mowgli, no!" Shanti cried. But Mowgli had already run off, with Shere Khan in hot pursuit.

"Ranjan, wait here," she said. "I've got to go help Mowgli."

Ranjan did as she said—for about two seconds. As he followed the others, he ran into Baloo.

"Where's Mowgli?" Baloo asked the boy.

Ranjan pointed. "Shere Khan!"

"Shere Khan? Hold on!" Setting Ranjan on his shoulders, Baloo rushed to the rescue.

Mowgli was still doing his best to stay ahead of Shere Khan. He reached the ruins of an ancient city and hurried into a giant theater to find a hiding place.

A second later, Shere Khan appeared. The tiger glanced around. The theater was silent and still.

"No matter how fast you run, no matter where you hide, I will catch you," Shere Khan said with a growl. "Come out, come out, wherever you are!"

As Baloo and Ranjan searched for Mowgli, they ran into Bagheera. The panther was startled to see another Man-cub.

"Take the kid, Baggy," Baloo panted, handing Ranjan over to Bagheera when they reached the ruined city. "I'll help Mowgli."

"Baloo!" Bagheera called. "Be careful!"

Baloo nodded. Then he crept into the theater.

While Shere Khan prowled nearby, Baloo quietly searched for Mowgli. Suddenly, Baloo heard a noise. He slowly rounded a corner and ran right into—Shanti!

"*You!*" they both cried.

They started to argue. Then they realized they were both there for the same reason—to help their friend.

"All right," Baloo said to Shanti. "You go that way. I'll cover you."

While Baloo and Shanti each hid behind a giant gong, Mowgli dove behind another one. The three friends tricked Shere Khan by taking turns banging the huge disks. Soon the confused tiger was running in circles, chasing the sounds.

Suddenly Shanti's gong fell over, revealing her hiding place. Mowgli jumped out to save her.

Shere Khan's eyes narrowed. "No more games, Man-cub."

Mowgli and Shanti ran away as Baloo tried to distract Shere Khan. But the tiger ran past Baloo and chased Mowgli and Shanti onto a ledge overlooking a pit of boiling lava.

Shere Khan roared as he closed in. The Man-cub was about to be his!

Baloo ran toward them as the tiger charged. "Mowgli, look out!" the bear cried.

As Shere Khan leaped at them, Mowgli and Shanti jumped across the lava pit onto a giant stone statue. Shere Khan followed, but his weight was too much for the crumbling stone. The statue collapsed and they all tumbled down, heading straight for the bubbling pit!

Luckily, Baloo stretched his giant paw down just in time to grab Mowgli and Shanti.

Mowgli and Shanti looked down to see that Shere Khan had landed on a stone pedestal surrounded by lava. The tiger was trapped!

A few minutes later, Mowgli watched sadly as Shanti and Ranjan were reunited with their parents. He looked at Baloo.

Suddenly, Mowgli knew where he belonged.

"Oh, Baloo," Mowgli murmured sadly.

Baloo guessed what was coming. "It's okay, kid," he said. "Go on."

Mowgli stared at his old friend. "Really?"

Baloo nodded. Mowgli grabbed him, burying his face in the bear's warm fur. They hugged for a long moment.

"I'm gonna miss you, Papa Bear," Mowgli said.

"Me too, Li'l Britches," Baloo replied with a sniffle. "Me too."

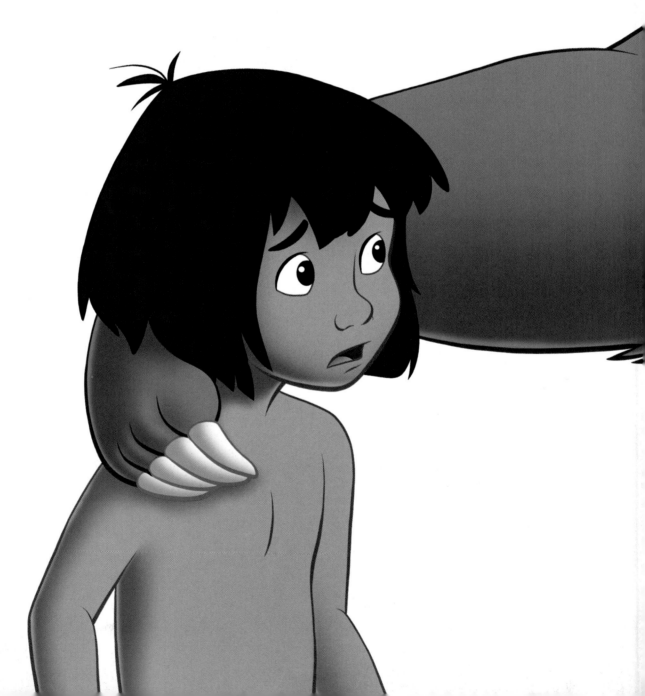

Back at the Man-village, life went on as usual. Well—*almost* as usual.

"Come on, Mowgli," Shanti called. "We'll be late!"

Mowgli grabbed a large water jug. "I'm right behind you."

They told the grown-ups they were going to fetch water. Then they raced to the river and skipped across the rocks to the jungle side. Ranjan popped out of Mowgli's jug.

"Let's remember to actually bring back some water," Mowgli said to the others.

As they drummed on the empty jugs, Baloo emerged from the jungle.

"Hiya, Papa Bear!" Mowgli called happily.

Soon Bagheera appeared, too. Ranjan hopped onto the panther's back as Baloo, Mowgli, and Shanti danced to the jungle rhythms.

Mowgli was finally where he belonged—with *all* his friends!